M O N I Q U E F

THE COLORS

CREATIVE EDITIONS
MANKATO

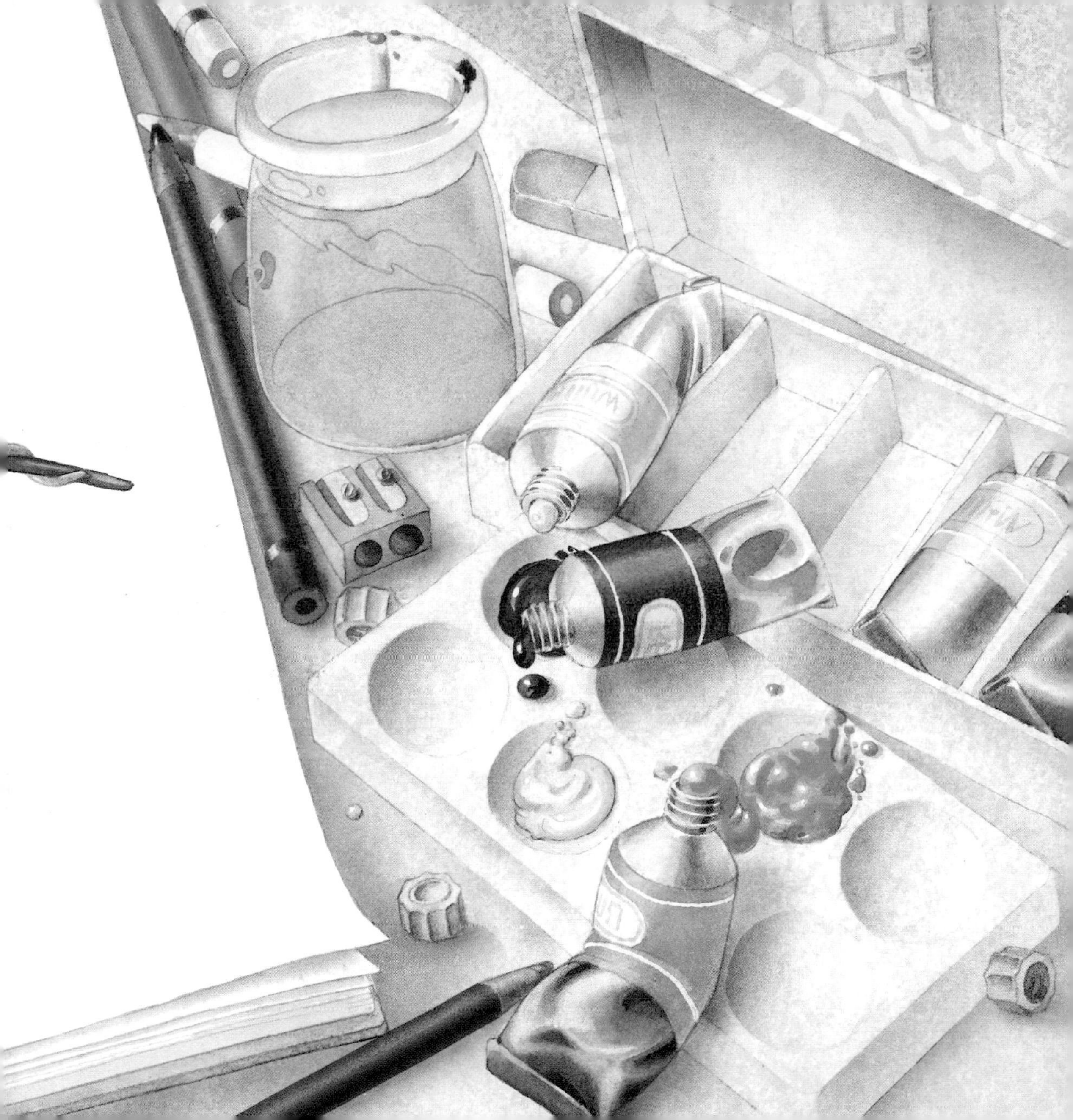

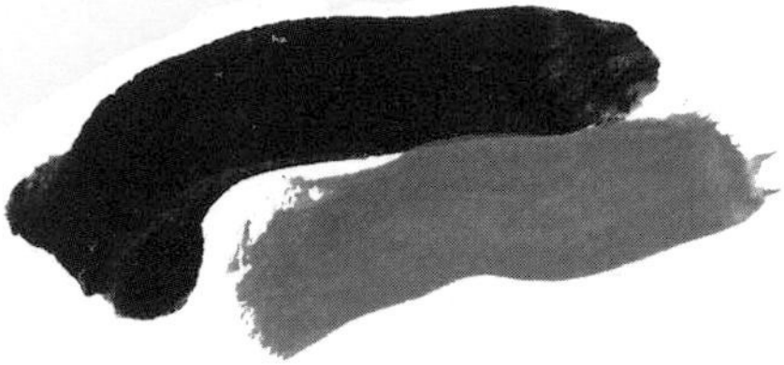

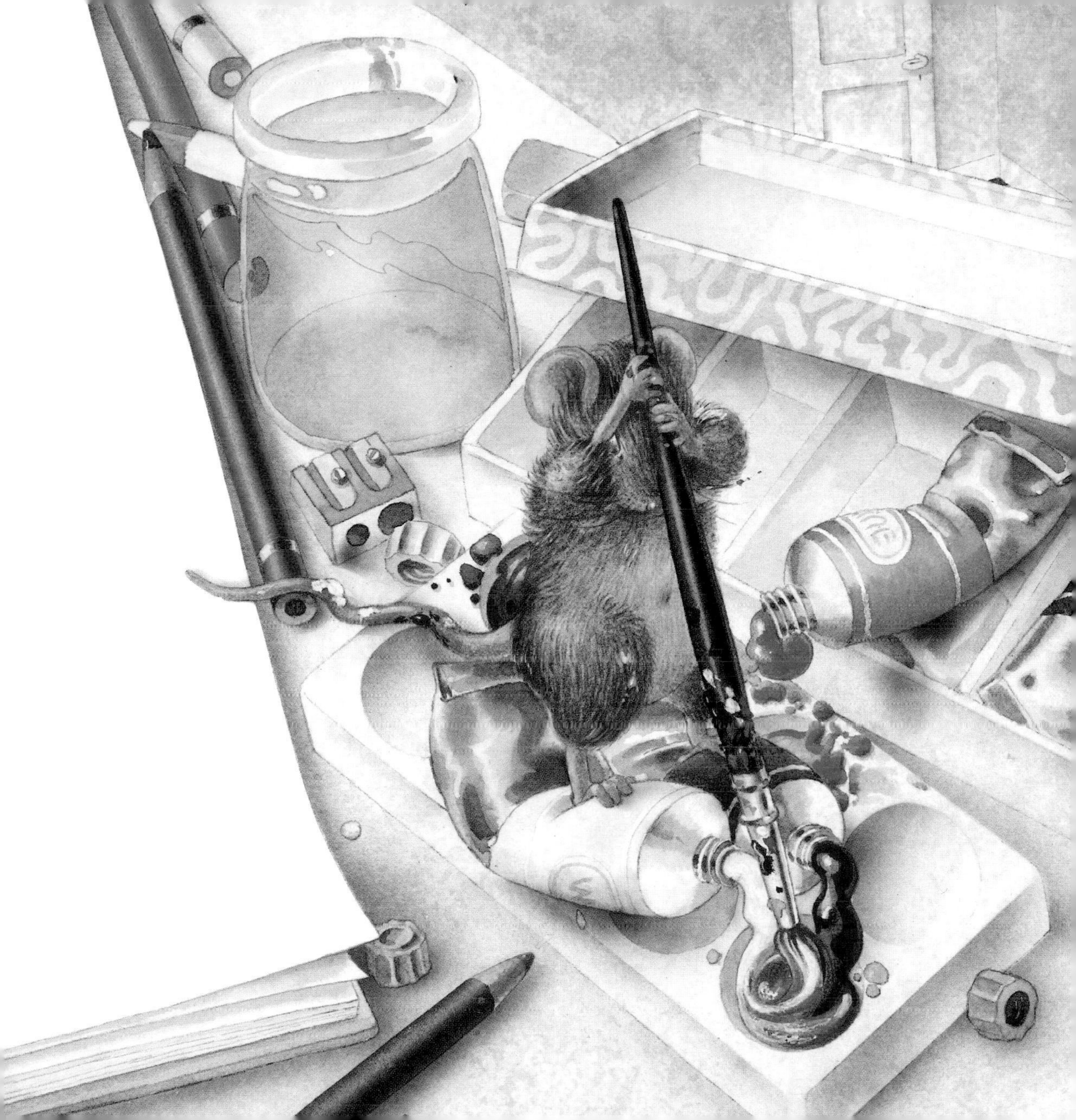

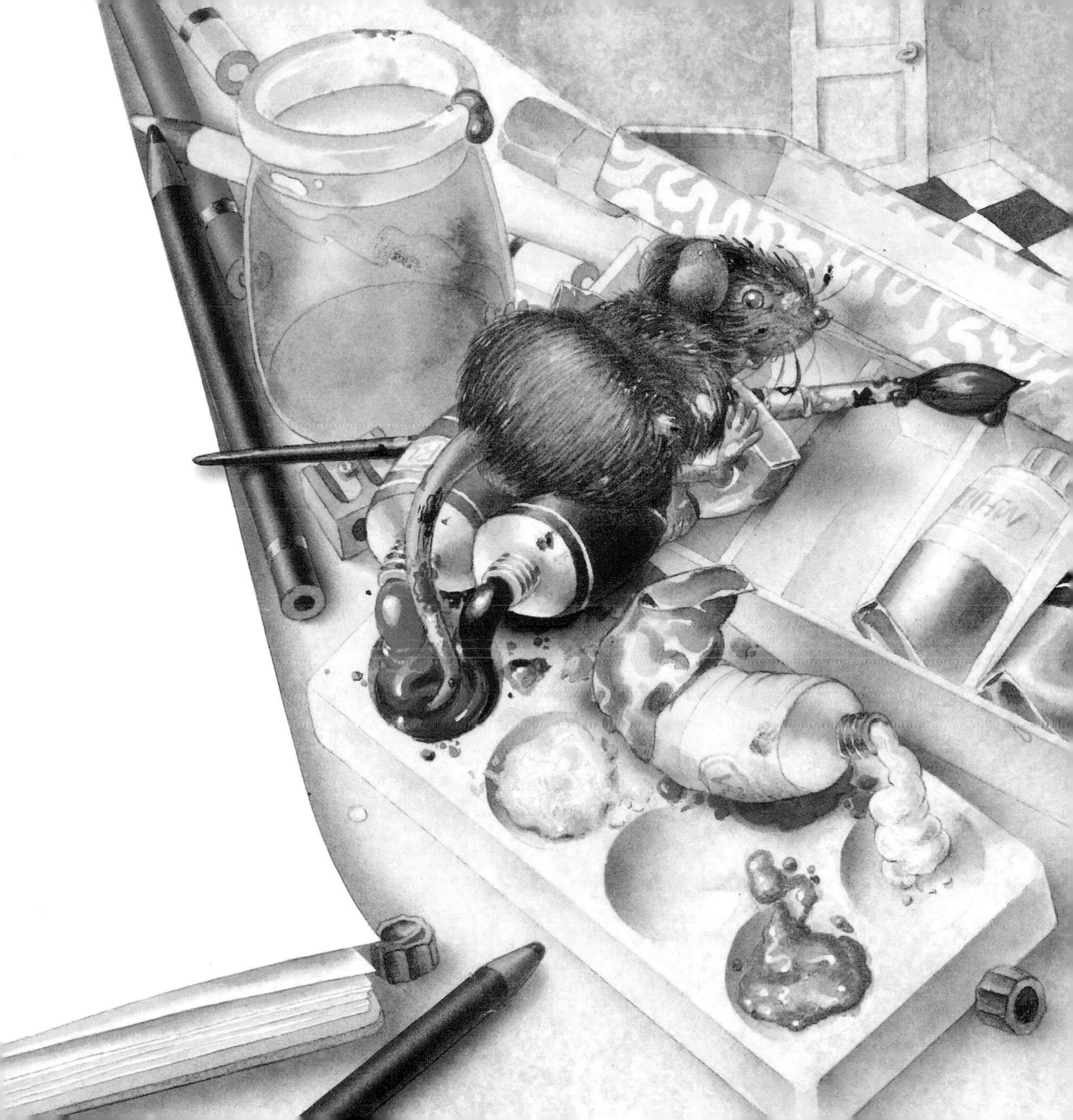

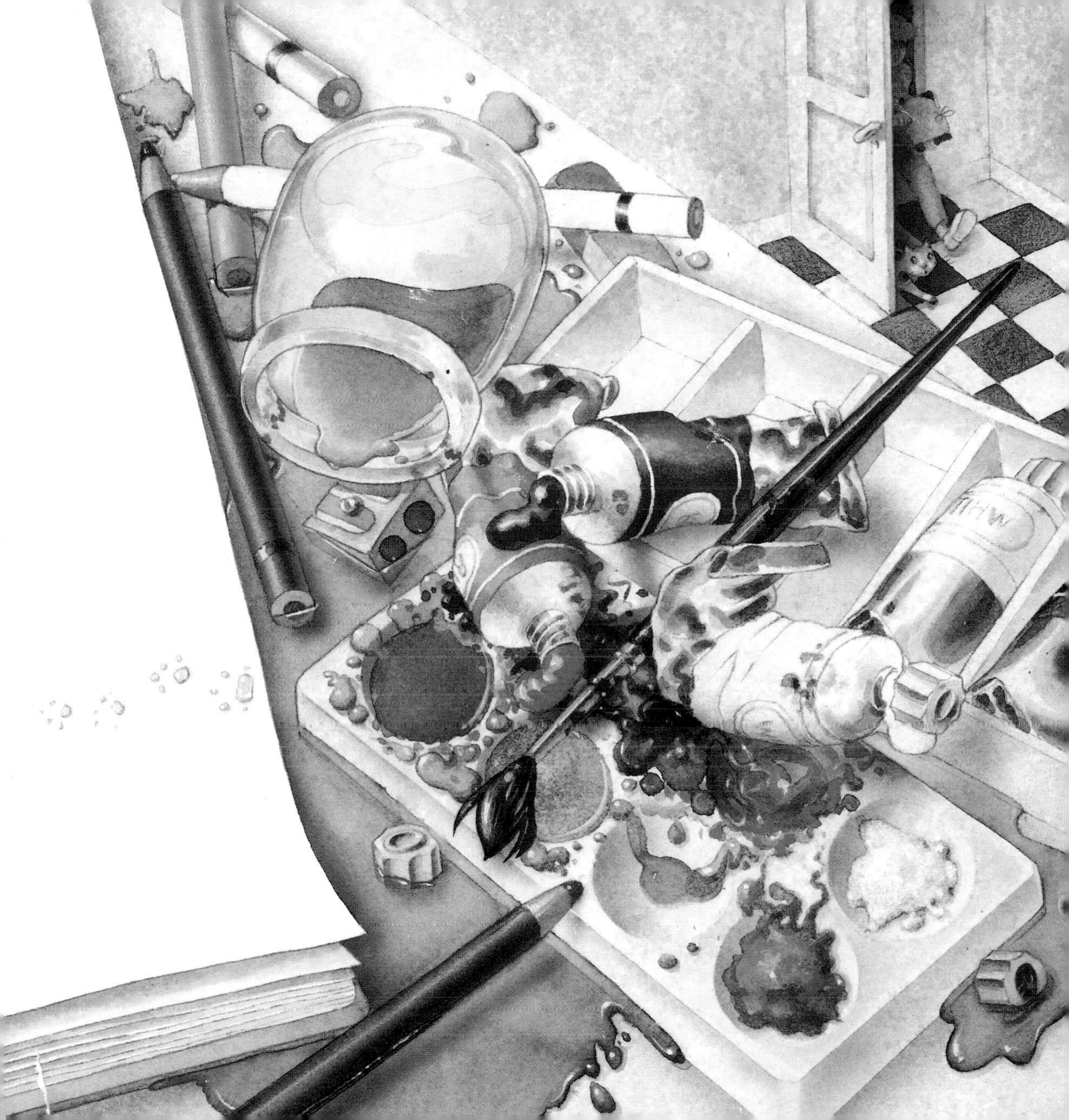